Little Bit India—Little Bit U.S.A.

These remarkable poems come from a remarkable woman. A member of several major organizations, she was born in Lucknow, India. She began writing—and succeeding at it—at an early age, winning the All-India Youth Festival and All-India Radio Play Awards.

For a time, still in India, she helped edit children's pages of the Bombay newspaper *Nava Bharat Times*.

Then Ms. Vira moved to the United States and earned a B.A. in Journalism and an M.A. in Economics and International Relations from the University of Colorado at Boulder. The University nominated her as one of the "Ten Outstanding American Women." In 1990, she was nominated for Who's Who Worldwide.

After her Colorado years, Ms. Vira gained a Ph.D. in International Relations and Economic Development from New York University, receiving at graduation the Founder's Day Award. Simultaneously, she served as a lecturer with the Speakers Bureau of the United Nations.

In addition to those duties and her continued writing, she has served in several ethnic organizations: as membership director and member of the Board of Trustees of the Association of Indians in America, and as Founder-Organizer Committee member of the Global Organization of People of Indian Origin, Inc.

She is active in the writing/marketing organization, Sisters in Crime, the Science Fiction and Fantasy Writers of America, the Freelancers Association, The Alliance of Global Business Exchange, the International Small Business Consortium, the Asian American Writers Workshop, the Small Press Center, and the National Writers Union, as well as a number of Internet groups including SFF.Net.

She owns and operates Vira Insurance Protection Services in New York City.

Also by Dr. Soma Vira

Transparencies Lean On
Poetry collection, Hartwick Electronic Press, 1994

Earth Trap: Rings Around the World
Novel, Space Link Books, New York, 1996
National Publishing House, New Delhi, 1992

Planet Keepers I: Checkmating Aliens
Novel, Space Link Books, New York, 1996

Planet Keepers II: Good Bye Alien God
Novel, Space Link Books, New York, 1996

Planet Keepers III: Nikita's Shadows
Novel, Space Link Books, New York, 1996

Planet Keepers IV: Lord Kito's Revenge
Novel, Space Link Books, New York, 1996

Kuru Trap, The Forbidden Blood
Novel, Space Link Books, New York, 1997

Angel Trails, Double Lives
Novel, Space Link Books, New York, 1996

Tinni
Novel, Kitab Mahal, Allahabad, India

Dharati Ki Beti
Short story collection, Alma Ram & Sons, New Delhi

Parchaiyon Ke Prashn
Short story collection, National Publishing House, New Delhi

Do Aankhon Vale Chehre
Short story collection, National Publishing House, New Delhi

Saathi Hath Badhana
Radio and stage play collection, Alma Ram & Sons, New Delhi

Little Bit India—Little Bit U.S.A.

Poems from East and West

by Soma Vira

Space Link Books

SECOND EDITION

Published by Space Link Books
New York, N.Y.

Manufactured in the United States of America
ISBN 0-9646057-3-2

Library of Congress Catalog Card No.: 96-071651

Publisher's Cataloging in Publication

Vira, Soma.
Little bit India, little bit U.S.A. : living in two worlds, from India to the U.S.A. / Soma Vira.
p. cm.
ISBN 0-9646057-3-2

I. Title.

PS3572.I73L58 1997 811'.54
QBI96-40712

To:

The Space Age Banyan tree like life forms (who
despite dear, Ol' Kipling)
make "The Twain" meet:

<u>In the "EAST" and "WEST":</u>

Mr. Chandra Pal Gupta, President,
Varshney Prakashan, Bombay, India
and
Dr. Robert F. Goheen (retired)
Ambassador to India, USA

Images Linking Fingers of Time
(Authors Note)

Soma the student: Waiting at the cutting edge of the coming-in seventies' beckoning career apertures.

New York University knocking at the *Greenwich Village.* Each day a new challenge. Dreaming images walking all around. In class rooms. Libraries. The Washington Square. The espresso spilling cafes. Lean bodies. Lanky, sturdy legs. Wide, strong shoulders, supporting long arms armed by passionately waving fingers, earnestly explaining an' re-explaining the universe, in expressive prose, poetry-teachers-horrifying-poems, and all the other *languages* in between.

So, what is one to do! Join them. Be them. Imagine their loves, passions, ambitions, and quarrels, and sing about them as if they were your own. Recite them to the accompaniment of rhythm riding animated spoons. Applause. Shouts of more...more...again...again. And, on top of it, get paid for that amateurish recitation by a beaming cafe-owner. Wow!

And, then, friends begin to urge. "Why don't you publish them?" Why not, indeed. Willing hands and minds select from the hand-scribbled piles. A book is born: *Little Bit India—Little Bit U.S.A.* My own, first book, in my adopted country! Wow! And, wow!

Soma the student: Dipping fingers in the whirlpools of publishing beckoning the twenty-second century.

New York City. A totally new territory for their aspiring-to-be-a-publisher-author. Criss-crossing long avenues proudly displaying its Barnes & Nobles, Daltons, and Doubledays. Joining new associations, Science Fiction and Fantasy Writers of America, Sisters in Crime, etc., etc. making new friends. Surfing their web sites. "Oh, Melisa," said to Melisa C. Michaels of the SFF.Net, "On your site, I found your fascinating sonnets. In the company of SF writers I never mentioned I also write poems because I thought..."

Why? Said the distinguished writer. *Check others' pages. There are many poets amongst us.* Checked, and delighted, posed a question, *Should I try to publish a collection of SFF.Net poets' poems?* With my blessings, said Jim MacDonald and Jeffry Dwight, the first-and-foremost SFWA poet. Great! said the awakened Spacebird Soma. But, that'd take time. Meanwhile...

As if the Never-Sleeping-Never-Forgetful Time was watching. The Time currents were listening. Linking the vast space, came BookWorld's Ronald T. Smith's ringing voice, Little Bit India *can be in our next catalog. But, it needs a new cover. ISBN numbers...*

"So, what are we waiting for! Let's do it," said Soma the Nightingale (or, Spacebird. But, that is another story to be revealed in the waiting-in-the-wings, *Trap* sequel, *Twin Trap, Swords from Space).*

So, here they are, my friends. The re-born images. All yours. To be critiqued. Torn apart. And, perhaps, have a tiny place on your book-shelf. Not mine any more. All yours.

Contents

I. To Catch...

Transparencies Lean On 3
Because 4
Won't You Please... 5
In the Lone Mirror 6
Sometimes 8
Ode to the Modern City 10
Water 12
Of All the Splendid Things 14
On Perfect Vacation 15
Not a Matter for a Computer 17
At a Poetry Reading 18
On the Eastern Wall 21
To Love (with Numbers?) 23
My Black-plumed Bird 24
Batik Thoughts 26

II. To Hold...

Vagabond 29
Memory 30
Untying the Wrappings 32
This Time of Morning 33
Moon over Mahalaxmi 35
Dream 42
For the Sake of Life 43
A Single Leaf's Falling 45
To JFK 47
Jai Jawan; Jai Kisan 52
A Rose for You *Chacha Nehru* 53
Departure 57
To a Midnight Dream 59
Tomorrow Is Not Far Away 61
Rainbow Knocks at Midnight 62

III. To Let Go...

Silence 67
Today 68
The Shadow 69
With—Without 70
The Reversed Roles 71
Beyond Understanding 72
The Niagara Falls 75
Only the Fish 76
In Tomorrow's *Rouge et Noir* 77
In the Footprints of Nowhere 79
To the End of the Red-Hot Street 80
Let the Fire Rage 82
Unadorned 83
To a Stone Carving 84
To Remember 85

IV. To Go With...

Sound without End 89
Door to the Deep Ocean 90
The Man Named Yesterday 91
Sense or Nonsense 93
An Ode to Our heartland 94
Ode to the Four-Year-Old 99
It Needs Only Two 101
To Julie and Jim 107
That Night 109
Until 110
No Matter How Many Time-Curtains 111
A Song for Sunlight 112
Nightingale Needs No Sidewalks 113
Little Bit India—Little Bit U.S.A. 115
Voila Tout 116

Little Bit India—Little Bit U.S.A.

I

To Catch...

...Agesilaus being invited once to hear a man who admirably imitated the nightingale, he declined, saying he had heard the nightingale itself.

—Plutarch, A.D. 46–120

Transparencies Lean On

Night leans on
the walls
lean on the legs

transparencies
lean on

an entire showcase moving
nowhere
as a storm riding the
planet earth

her
paint-tubes undone, brushes
limp, an empty rose hanging
outside
the hollow stove

two sculptures: metal and wood
balance on the upturned floor

and Picasso squats on
the canvas of the
picture of the room

Time
is transparent—an
invisible smell that maddens
the *Kasturi mrag**—smell it as
you think it
speeds past.

* A rare species of deer that carries a precious herb, *Kasturi*, in its navel. It is said that, excited by its perfume, the deer searches for it all over the forest, and does not know till the day of its death that the herb is hiding in its own body.

Because

1.

the cloud looks so beautiful
because the twilight holds it
tenderly as an adolescent
her first bouquet...

2.

the rainbow curves
because the refugee raindrops
have kidnapped for ransom
sky and dawn—the insatiable
newlyweds...

3.

so patiently flows the river
because the moon clutches it—
emulating eagerly the vivacity
of a child's hungry lips...

Won't You Please...

Life:
a tourniqueted door
—pleated obliquely
    by waste paper
        bonds;
someone said, "Open Sesame,"
and
a sweepstakes number walked in.

            Life:
    —a breathing boat
stamped with serialized
    registered
    bonus number;
        i said,
    "Shut in Sesame,"
    the door closed
  but
  the Number walked out
  for
  the petty-cash window
      remained open.

The innings coughed
only once lightly
  lifted the tourniquet and
  said: "Won't you, please,
      shuffle the cards."

In the Lone Mirror

O Sky!
Don't be so jealous!

Don't look down
so cravingly on the
lone mirror
in my room,
which until a few
minutes ago
was empty
as you
are
without
Your Moon.

But, is now
reflecting
the iridescent
circumference,
of something new,
glowing like
a thousand
fugitive
moons.

(and seems capable of
enslaving all the
senses of a
Bhishma and
a Rome)

Believe me, O Sky!
I've not stolen your
Moon.
What you're seeing
in my mirror is the
gift of the year
—life's fragrance
placed upon my
intoxicated table
by
someone like
the roving Knight
of
The Lady of the Lake.

Sometimes

three a.m.
the Crazy Horse Cafe
stretches and yawns. Only
  (take it easy, partner
    the night is still young)
because
sometimes
sitting in the subterranean hole
      drinking espresso, or
      coffee
the mind acquires the complexion
and consistency
of vapid liquid
in a revolving cup
  (to your feet...to your feet...
      shake it up).
But,

this is not the real life. No, of
course not.
Only a few hours does one
devote
to such soundless pursuits;
for the most part one thinks of
Euripedes, Tchaikovsky, or
    Martin Luther King
and the glass is filled with
    Chivas Regal
(or, something like that), and
sometimes, he or she (the
living protege
of Eros or Aphrodite)
unhooks the knees and unbends
the arms

to lay them flat on the
table top; and expounds
at l e n g t h
all about Schopenhauer, Sartre,
        or, Spinoza...
and to listen gravely surround
them the sketches on
tables, chairs and walls (reminders
of an Herculean
age of Art
        that cannot
        be equalled in
        technique, or, thought).

And,
surrounded by such a groovy atmo-
sphere one admires
silently almost (by Jove) seriously
the talents of minds and fingers
  —pleased
with the unequalled genius of
one's space moving idea generation;
     sometimes
     one wonders:
     how is it that he and i
     —the two of *us*—
so unlike him and her (the old ones),
     can be so defiantly
        rational...
        and so...profound!

Ode to the Modern City

You, Modern City:

With your great glass Phoenix eyes staring at the burning Sun without any pity—

What devilish scheme

Are you now fabricating to make me feel that be it darkness or light, every single breath i exhale is your slave, and *only* you are supreme?

You, proud Sorceress:

Who told you—you can lay down massive labyrinthine wilderness, from whose unblessed, comfortless, carcass, i can *never* find an egress?

Your unsullied Belief

Has *no* lusty limbs to stand upon, for long before you were born, the lonely God in His grief twisted His thumb and planted in my honey-gold system, a pattern of arteries, running like empty rivers towards oceans of splashing silver, but anchored all the time to rock-like boundaries carved in a floating reef.

With some sanity and desire to listen

You can hear my dark, humane, processes going on about their "wrap-it-up-in-a-day" business—call them Desire, Will, Volition, Passion, Cognition, or Conation, they all keep busy constantly, like the billion fingers of a million *Ravanas*—carrying on with the protoplasmic body *as if* it was a soon-to-be-perfected violin.

You think, you can reduce me

To the position of your helpless, wordless, dutiless machine—when i'm getting exhausted trying to circumnavigate endlessly, focussing my wind-torn compass at oblique corners of the thorn-strewn fields of experiences?

O you Cruel, Cloistered, Beauty:

No matter how hard you try, you *cannot* reach me (the proof is in your mirror—in where, from whichever angle you look, you'll see, *not* your face, *but* mine) for i'm the *only* perennial City.

Water

Were you
given
birth in anger and fury;
then embraced
with naked—Love;
giving Peace?
Security?
Did you then
secretly pray
—tremulously asking
for ornamental things—
unbridled manhood and womanhood sweet
(strength like fire;
pity like Stones and Sand
—hidden in caves
of Virginity:
pure Lust)?

Is that
why
leave you untouched,
unharmed,
(without rhyme or reason)
pains which
paralyse?
Is that
why
your dreams are thunders
—desires bridled
only awaken
storms dying with thirst;
and slumber and
silence
spell only
one epigram:
"Shadow yours prisons life Mine.
Must it live?"

You were
given
Fury and Anger in birth.
Embraced then
Love—naked with
Peace. Giving
Security.
Then, you did
pray secretly.
asking tremulously
things ornamental for
sweet womanhood and manhood unbri
—fire like Strength;
sand and stones, like Pity
(caves in hidden
virginity of
pure Lust).

That is
why
untouched you leave,
unharmed,
reason or rhyme (without
which pains
paralyse).
That is
why
thunders are dreams—your
bridled desires
awaken only
thirst with dying storms;
and slumber and
silence
only spell
epigram one:
"Mine life prisons yours shadow.
Live it must."

Faceless, merciless Sanity. You
eternal O
Endless—You Water—
(life in Everything
everywhere),
your perpetuity
means
Death revolving Eternity
and
steps following steps.

You—Sanity merciless, faceless
O eternal
Water. You, endless;
(everything in life
everywhere),
perpetuity your
means
Eternity revolving Death
and
steps following steps.

Of All the Splendid Things

Of all the splendid things that
Shakespeare wrote,
this passage from *Macbeth*
i like to quote:
    And pity, like a naked new-born babe,
    Striding the blast, or heaven's cherubim, horsed
    Upon the sightless couriers of the air,
    Shall blow the horrid deed in every eye...

These words seem to have immortal wings,
(like *Garuda's** plume) and to them clings
a hush of Freedom, Hurry, and Suspense—
Something the opposite of Nonchalance.

But, hunters are we, with colored glass eyes
turning shadows to truth; and truth to lies.

Our shield is Vanity (tangled like seaweed)
and from its glorious eternal seed
we learn *Everything* about
Power, Death and Money (how to
inflate punctured peace and dissect
lonesome Harmony),

And in odd moments Shakespeare makes me think:
—if Sanity sees us, would she shrink?
and would it prompt Her to leave Her slumber
to be a *Courier in the air* with spiked spur?

    Would then Tyranny shrivel, go
    unrolling under Her heavy heel
    and Hate-Superiority venoms come calling
    to spice Her mid-day meal?

Oh, Yes! "Striding the Blast," that
    sounds great.
        But,
        What If
        Sanity
            wakes up
                too late?

* Garuda is God Vishnu's celestial courier.

On Perfect Vacation

(To my grandfather, Raja Shri Fakir Chanda, I.S.E.)

Nothing
can stop him when he
  wants to leave his
  chair
  to sit
  under the Sun...

fishing
hour after hour he waits
not remembering
  he has a strict
  routine which
dictates his presence
near glass-jars-full-of
steaming bio-chem stuff
without which
  he doesn't feel like
  a living man...

looking
and listening he sits and
  the willows whistle
  and the birds
  hop over his
  toes and
  his thoughts
    wander...

dwelling
upon facts known and
unknown—fear and
hate...mosquitoes and
antibiotics...love and
misery and atomic
fission and
  supervision...

all
of which (droning in
his mind) wanting to
  check his reactions
  toward the
  performance
  of their tasks (in
the name of protecting,
safeguarding, *everyone's*
Past-Present-and-Future...

Bowing
low, the Sun reminds him
  —it's time to go
and with a half-drawn
  sigh he
  tears himself from
  his preferred,
  selected world, in
    one whole piece...

Pulling
his pole he prepares to
return home—to his
anxious wife
  —a dutiful husband and
  a careful scientist
  who at the
  moment
  does not
    know

that
  ...the river has
carried away his shoes and
    his hook
    is still
      unbaited.

Not a Matter for a Computer

A computer can count
but
  ...not always...

when the snow-flake floats down
to lean upon the lonely dunes,
miles liquefy
like punctured balloons...

when the river dives down to
dip in the dandy ocean,
miles solidify
like a Cleopatra's vision...

when at a center (Rockefeller)
one waits for the elevator creak,
miles multiply
like steps to an untouched peak...

and when the distance thus
lingers, loiters, labors,
Mind's groovy programmer
coolly prints out the words:

—sixty billion miles are
  shorter than a step in
  the elevator (or two
  across the door)...won't you
ever know—distance is not a
matter
  for a wall-clutching
computer...must you
        stand at the shore?

At a Poetry Reading

we stand
talking to others in the penthouse whose walls
are the colors (like tiger's skin under an umbrella of black ivory) of nude
    paintings—black, yellow and white—pasted as if for ever;
the captions beneath them flooded with
long-drawn
            titles.

i talk
to him; you talk to her (the bright chandelier burns above like the Forbidden
    Apple prodding
    the snake)
—and in this fully-clothed enclosure,
we drift apart breathing as in
an airtight Mariner II orbiting
the square earth.

i tell him
about my poems; you tell her about your books
(your name floats to me; mine to yours; stringing
melodies deep
into ears' hollowness; folding and molding
        the icicles of memory)—holding
  and upholding each other thus
  we sail off towards
  our strange chairs.

our strange chairs
hold our bolted bodies; but our eyes sail (and
sail again, solidifying the image [sensational] of a
thought)—and under the curious glare of the solid
chandelier we locate a star in the
land-of-nowhere. But, the currents of space
shred apart
to open the window of aught, and suddenly
                                        there's
                                            Silence.

the poet
reads from his published works (his
words rotate against the tiger-skin walls);
the curtains of our windows blow
in and out
in and out
to reveal the snake
rising.

my wings
are ticking conventions; yours bright doubts (they flap in the orbit with full
turn-overs) that blind
the snake
—who
makes one
last
effort
with deep wrath; dethrones
the doubts
firing a slinging swish of
its loping, ubiquitous
tail.

we float.
the Mariner clings to our compelling feet (beneath is the sky fed upon thirsty
colors) and
conch-shells of laughter
rippling with waves upon waves of Black Mary,
Gin, and rollicking Vodka
slip softly
to our
star-anchored, moon-shadowed
wings.

we come
together to the tiger-skin walls (facing each other)
facing shadows on the wall a child's arms
yearning—reaching upwards—to circle
a tall Elm; whispering whispering:
"You are beautiful...beautiful..." and
together
we say goodbye (me to him and you to her)
—thinking: they are modern, these
Forbidden Apples. They cannot
introduce us
—the two strangers—
to each other.

On the Eastern Wall

January One-Nineteen-Sixty-Four
  —two hours to morning, and
a new Calendar
on the eastern wall.
Logic says: it's
New Year. A new dawn is breaking.

But,
can i believe it? Can i believe it
without seeing the Shadow that
should cross the street to throw
light upon
          the Calendar's
soon-to-be-bygone face?

And, standing here *now*
between the open window and closed
walls; in complete darkness surrounded
by far-away fireworks; do i
like it—this Sputnik of memories
hurtling, not in space, but in between
  this morning and *that* night?

Do i dare ask these eyes suspended
in the mirror: "Was Yesterday
yours? Will you be able to take
Tomorrow?"..."Will you be
happy to know—
                    someone is thinking of
you

(not as you were in '63. not as you
will be in '64, but)
as you are *now*
suspended in space ticking
like Time depending
upon the Shadow that *should* cross
the street to throw light upon the
Calendar's
soon-to-be-bygone face

two hours from now..."

To Love (with Numbers?)

"You loved me
                    once why
can't you
                    NOW?"

"I do
      not
            k...n...o...w"

"Remember? We had pro-
mised   to
                love
till e
      t
       e
        r
         n
          i
           t
            y
         b
      u
   t
it has been only thirty
hours!"

"Do you have to be
     like all the others?"

"Whatdoyu mean?"

"Needling...needling
              to
     shorten "eternity"
                    with numb-
ers?"

My Black-plumed Bird

I adjust my glasses and look again
—look again and look again.
But I do not see
Flotilla—my black-feathered bird
With its funny little hop and
Funny little jump
Circling my canvas, paints and
brush and me.

Its feathers had shiny scales
—as if it was a black mermaid.
and with its crimson throat and
Naked feet,
It floated from tree to tree,
Like a black rose poised
In the hands of a fairy
Swinging on ropes of spree.

Often like a child prodigy
—wanting to astonish me,
It added to its low flight
An extra circle and swoop,
With a wider loop,
So that it seemed
As if in this universe,
Only two things were important:
This black-feathered bird
And its roving tree.

It knew when I did not want to be
                    disturbed, and it mimed
A silent 'copter, flying
Without least effort,
Both backward and forward,
As if to say:
I am a picture.
A beautiful picture.
Catch me. Catch me.

My moods changed.
                    But it knew, ever and always.
And its flights and songs
Were high, low, or stationary
According to the limpid
Curves of my thoughts at the moment
Plaguing me.

I wonder, and look again:
                    where can it be and why
The absence of such a small thing
Has left behind
Such a vast emptiness
Rolling and rolling
Upwards and downwards and all-around,
Without any mercy.

From Caravan *magazine,*
New Delhi, India

Batik Thoughts

Sunday morning
sleepy sunshine
slips in—tiptoes around
blazing *batik* thoughts*
on spellbound, speechless
walls
like lacquered shadows
left behind
by your acoustic,
    unscribbled
                    presence.

* Batik is a colorful tie-dye painting done on a special type of cloth.

II
To Hold...

...They spoke, I think, of perils past,
They spoke, I think, of peace at last.
One thing I remember:
Spring came on forever,
Spring came on forever,
Said the...nightingale.

—Nicholas Vachel Lindsay, 1879–1931

Vagabond

The clouds
　　up above. So pretty.
Seem today

　　—almost green
as they look down
upon the shrugging hills
　　refusing to give
　　to the belligerent wind
　　their virgin trees...

A wild squirrel
drinks from a low,
　　leaf-lined hollow
　　lying
　　at a Chestnut's trunk,
and wisps of songs from
sky-bound birds
　　float softly
　　through the dense forest
　　attired
　　with shadows and moss...

Here i belong,
　　the vagabond
　　mind craves
　　for these things—alive and
　　free
while Life is fettered,
　　chained,
　　to the passion torn,
　　love-drenched city...

Memory

(To Kakra—our village that lives
like the Ganges and the Himalayas)

Near the end of the village,
the narrow path bends
to kiss the creek and
extend
two thin arms
to support
the towering
ridge.

Cupped in the nook of its elbow,
sheltered by a wild flower fence
(colors stolen from a rainbow—
the flowers dropped
by Heaven one by one),
a simple, unadorned temple
marks the existence
of Krishna—the God Who once
came to live with men.

There are no names on the walls;
but, they say:
Once when the Times were precarious
(a War raged in a far-off place,
conscription was heavy. only
old hands were left to till
the land. And the Draught
was raging thirsty and hungry
to meet his wife,
the dust-veiled
Famine),
the children gathered

in the nook, fashioned
the image of Krishna—the Child Divine;
bowed their heads; closed their eyes;
and without
eating

without
          sleeping
prayed for seven days and
                seven nights;
and on the eighth day the Sun could not
                leave
                the womb of the Night
                for Krishna came riding
                upon dark, threatening,
                            omnivorous,
                                        Clouds.

War
     was
          ended.

The victorious
villagers came back built
the Temple cemented
with love
          (of Life and Rhythm
               dancing eternally
               in the deeds of
               the Divine Child).
They did not
leave their names

but
during the summer days
   and long winter nights,
the winds from the Himalayas
            sweep down
          to shower benediction
upon those who in legacy
received not gold, silver,
        or
        diamonds undying,
        but only
                 Memory.

And the tattered village—
       fenced by wild flowers,
continues to survive. Keeps on
                  breathing.

Untying the Wrappings

The Lightning has not yet
folded its wings
and the storm is still
raging;
but, tonight, i'll sleep
for
under my pillow

is your gift;
and i'm going to dream
about your hands
untying the
wrappings and the strings

releasing
the taut antelope
to let it grope for and find
its sheltered grotto
in the storm-centered zone.

This Time of Morning

1.

This Time of Morning
the sandalwood-air is
  cool and fresh
and on the banks of the
Ganges, the temples
  sing:

  "Dingle-Ding. Ring-in.
Ring-in-the light that is
Shiva. The light that is Brahma.
For your body, composed of the
    (five basic elements)
Panchtatva, must ring in
satyam, shivam, sundaram.

2.

This Time of Morning
I'm the *Sky*
and I see:
    my inquisitive brain
prying without restrain
is the restless
          night
full of a *billion* burning
              lights.

3.

This Time of Morning
I'm the *Earth*
and I feel:
    my anchored heart
craving for the blazing trail
is the laboring
          day
lit with a burnished
              lamp

4.

This Time of Morning
I'm the *Wind*
and I say:
    my roving breath
dispelling the dread of love
is the swirling
                life
dancing with the weak-kneed
                        death.

5.

This Time of Morning
I'm the *Water*
and I cry:
    the night has a billion eyes;
    the day *only* one.
Yet, the light of the world dies
            with the dying sun.

6.

This Time of Morning
I'm the *Fire*
and I know:
    the mind has a billion fires
    the heart only *one.*
Yet, the light of the whole life dies
                when *love* is done.

Moon over Mahalaxmi*

(To my mother who called herself "Shanta")

Moon over Mahalaxmi
      (Rahu-Ketu** menaced Moon)—
where steps lead down to
the sea...where Life gropes and
neither birth
                    nor death
                              is supreme
...the waters wash against the
   sacred slopes and
   in disguise (wearing
                    elephant's
                    mask),
Devi Durga's secret agent,
                         wise Ganesha
keeps watch
                    listening
                    to the *Koyal's****
                         warning call.

Moon over the farmlands
      (white butterfly moon)—
where cottonseed mists
                         drift
among the gaily laughing *Tesu*
...mimicking, mocking, teasing,
   the high and mighty
                              Palash...

* Mahalaxmi Temple is one of the oldest and most precious temples, situated at the shore where the ocean's tides are higher and more fierce, dedicated to Goddess Laxmi in Bombay, India

** Twin demonic meteors chasing sun and moon, determined to imprison them in their mouths, causing eclipses.

*** Koyal is the Indian name for the nightingale.

softly,
whisperingly,
the white wings of moon butterflies
flicker d
                  o
                     w
                        n
upon thatched, torn
                roof tops,
painting upon
                          darkness

the freshly-twisted cotton wicks of
                        time tarnished candles.

—where the air
is full of fleeting perfumes and
sleepy
              jungle sounds,
on the fingered terraces
the
        reflecting outline
        of the moon
poses proudly as a silver floor
for the young
                        Wheat
                          and
                        Mustard tycoons
to sway and
                      dance upon...

and upon the low hillocks,
        where
                    glow-worms crown
the green fairies'
                    emerald tiaras,
a flute
illuminates
                    the bridge of darkness
                    upon which
                    with

beaming eyes
the lonely night
w
a
i
t
s
to welcome
her *Dauphin*, Dawn.

Moon over the cities
(carved Moon—caricature
of an unfinished bud)—
the unfinished moon
...opening its petals slowly
in the warmth of the Neon
lights dwarfing the light
of Red Fort, Kutub Minar,
Taj Mahal, Birla Temple and
all the rest like them...

...stopping (fixed on its unseen
stem for a while), where the
monkeys—mothers and their
young ones—sleep fearlessly
among the slumbering
branches, and the beggars
lie in the city corridors
huddled together...

the sun-flower
droops in its presence and the
carefully
sculptured
coconut palms
catch
little reflections and
pool them on
their leaves
like

gleaming anklets
d
a
n
c
i
n
g
in the feet of a
blissful
*devadasi.**

Moon over India
(watchful Moon—forging,
vanguarding the river
of *Bharat*-destiny—
where the sleepless,
sand-rimmed
burning eyes of the deserts,
and the untiring
shoulders
of the sky-cropping
mountains
ripen temperance
in its
beholden rays
...dream lanterns
linger dimly
thru life's uncut coals and
the
light in the willows
keeps on m
o
v
i
n
g
like the flashing of a
thousand silver *bulbuls***
thru dark shoals...

* a temple dancer

** small, colorful singing birds

—and where
the finely hewn
marbles of
beloved graves, mosques,
churches and pagodas
flash
unceasingly
like
sun-clipped
ripples,
thru velvet dusks
the intangible evening air
steals music
from
the moonstruck fountain's
pushing foams.

Moon over my binoculars
(unexplored Moon, hiding
treasures rare)—
and as i stand
at the temple gates
at cool of night, hearing
the rich, resonant
tones of
worshipful bronze
vibrating
thru the priest pillars,
beneath
dark
moss-lacquered
ancient domes
white pigeons
come winging home,
and i see
altar candles...flower
to flickering blossoms
incense fringed...the hanging
bells sliding away as if touched
by playful Diana's
swinging feet...

and peace
descending in
shimmering cascades
to capture
the F
U
G
I
T
I
V
E
code messages
carried by
the unearthly
light-beams.

—above me
the Sky
looks fleeced
like the glimmering
scales
of an unvanquished
*Matsya**
nodding its fins,
sometimes,
to say:
"you may know,
today and every tomorrow
*Rahu-Ketu*** will
n
e
v
e
r
be
victorious.

This Moon...Shiva-
Durga's Moon...
will

* The first incarnation of God Vishnu as a gigantic fish.

** Twin demonic meteors chasing sun and moon, determined to imprison them in their mouths, causing eclipses.

always
        win.
It will
rain on every nightfall."

Dream

the lacquered *Meenar*
rose
to us promising
together-darkness

wild with peace.
eloquent
like captivated dreams
garnished with wine and cheese
the fingers of flesh
felt the importance of earth
and silence
sent maddening verbs
to the two water-bucks
who reared and plunged
with deep understanding—

space
surrounded us
with such openness
that there was nothing
but Apollo's rowboat
caressing the valleys it made
softly—
the river-banks then smelled the song
i touched the Elysium with
and sliding over soft pebbles
the river heard the taste of your kiss.

For the Sake of Life

(To late Smt. Guru Ji)

Saints, Prophets, Messiahs, *Avatars**,
sprouting from a single seed
ached suffered bled to parse
matters Man must
heed

again and again
they bowed their heads
and said:

—despite everything as yet something
solid
throbs in Life.
Is this precious, ubiquitous little
breath
to be exploded in fear-hate and strife
for Birth to be merely the genesis of
Death?

Surely, Man can master something better
than being a wolf to fellow-men. So, why
not
let selfish motives,
mind, and matter
compose a tune
of rational regimen
to prove to none but yourselves
that you are something different
than a lion who has tasted
human blood.

* incarnations

They lived
to show as teacher, guide, and friend
that even dying Life
can be lived yet
                    like life
that means Life in both,
                              means and end;
that even untamed Life
can be lived yet
                           like life
that does not mean
                           Barbarity
bred on other's
                           toil and sweat.

for the sake of Life
again and again
            they bowed their heads
and blessed those who
dirtied their hands
         with their holy blood.

A Single Leaf's Falling

(To Raja Jawala Prashad,
who loved me like my own Grandfather)

My eyes stare thru the window of
my room and i ten thousand
decades away;
my vision is filled with Nature's
drums of doom
—storms and Foam and
stinging spray.
Let the drums roll for many a
Fire shall die.

Time's fire is dead;
and ashes mock the skies. The Sun
walks slowly; Moon is losing height.
Books slide down the shelves calling
them to rise but the night
throbs with shock and
the day
without light.
Let the drums roll for many a
Battle Ship shall die.

Battle Ship's corpse is tattered:
and dreams with gilded edge
shock the *Ahiravan's* eyes
for shackled arrows are shot to
shoot the slumbering, marble shark
and shelved upon Time's
moth-eaten ledge
knowledge weeps
—as does
Thunder in the dark.
Let the drums roll for many a
Grief shall die.

Grief's tears have marched away:
and those that are left in the
shrinking camp
tramp in the time-worn grooves

with a waltzing step, while
their bodies
grow wrinkles
like a much-used map.
Let the drums roll for many a
Flower shall die.

Flower's memory is buried:
and its grave covered by
a young leaf that i saw
falling
thru
my window-glass.
Let the drums roll for many a
Leaf shall die.

Leaf's life was cut short:
and the affluent tree stands.
But,
holding on to the splintering
Sun, the shadows
spotlight the Opposition's
gun— Why does a single leaf's
falling
make the Memory bleed?
Why does it explode the
worlds of a tattooed
mind and turn loose
the limbs never freed
into a bereft Power
no longer blind?

and the calm, peaceful, funeral pyre,
softly
answers
(softly whispers):
Let the drums roll for many a
Fire shall rise
...shall rise...

To JFK

(November 23, 1963)

Fastened to the summit of Life
a steel chord
laughing under the blue sky
has been snapped in mid-air
by
a Sniper's
bullet
and all the Languages of the world
are
sobbing
for they cannot
find the words
to describe
this
tragedy

It is *not* Rain that soaks
this Earth—Brown and
Black and
Yellow and
White...It is
water clouding
the eye
of the
world. And

the wind bearing the cloud
whistles
with pain:
Is it that every
generation
should share
the crime
of snuffing out
the Candle.

(the Candle that is born to burn)
with iron-like faith
and passion
to ship friendship and
compassion and overturn
cradles of fear to forget and
(unlearn)

Something America had learned
JFK...you were
the man amongst men...
—Father: chock-full of care
Husband: who loved to "accompany Jackie"
most precious
limb of a precious family—the
oldest surviving
brother.

Were you
too good;
too brave;
too kind; and
is that WHY
the Gods thought us
not fit for your company
and called you back
in the prime of your life?

Now, you belong to
two worlds—our own and
the Higher One.
And the coming centuries will
remember you
as we do
the other
Emancipators, like
...Buddha
Lincoln and
Gandhi
who breathed for people and

                    died
at the Cross of Ignorance.

Buddha smiled while he ate the
poisoned pudding; Gandhi greeted
his assassin with folded hands and
you
    waved and cheered before
    the bullet carried you away.
Oh! The human mind! How can it
conceive
        such unthinkable
                    crimes
...even the nuclear bombs would
be more bearable
                for one would
know that
          they are coming.

"Our ancestors," we say, "lived
in the 'dark ages'..."
True. They hanged from high
poles
    such special criminals;
so that
even the beasts among men
would know that
                man
                should not
                become
such a depraved, scheming animal.

But, we (according to us)
    are
civilized People. We do not
demean ourselves by *such*
dirty ways.
        We
prefer to treat a criminal
  —even a special one—
with a quick, easy sentence.

And
he dies
without
many even knowing
the hour
of his death.

Oh, yes! What *civilized* People
we are—What an astounding
Genius! What a creative Mind
we possess (haven't we invented
sputniks, weather satellites...);
but
we don't even have the mind to
create
a simple device
that'd
enable us to save a man's life
from one man's hand; and
tell everyone
in all the ages
that such a thing
"is
just
not
done."

And, we (above all)
are powerless to
invent
the Words
that'd
tell a mourning wife
how to inform her
three year old son and
six year old daughter
that Daddy won't be there
—ever—
to bring that birthday present.

. . .and
that'd
tell the
people
of so many nations
how to
tell
their
children
that
in the year
Nineteen Hundred and Sixty-
Three
at one p.m.
on Friday, November
Twenty-Second,
they lost a pious,
devoted
and
beloved
Leader.

Jai Jawan** : Jai Kisan****

(In memory of late Prime Minister Shri Lal Bahadur Shastri who gave this meaningful slogan to India)

Fierce though your loneliness
for the spongy street-walkers
—War-Upon and
Conquest...
i long to be your shadow
for your nearness
smells
of the wholesome
ripeness
of a protected
home;
and when i touch you
i see
the cliffs you were
quarried from.

slippery sometimes
though your step...my
kisan...my soldier
...soul of India,
soul of Time...
i know
if it wasn't
for you and your likes
instead of young lips
tasting
Rohu
there'd be nothing but
fish
and the jittery ocean
would be flowing over us
engulfing
Bharat Ma.

* Victory to...

** Term for a soldier (like here, for the police, we say, "our finest.")

*** farmer

A Rose for You *Chacha Nehru*

(To Shri Dharma Vira, I.C.S.
—the right hand of Late Prime Minister Nehru)

Uncle adorable
Chacha Nehru,
up there
somewhere
Kamla
waits
for you and
here
the world's
sorrow
—like a
Kohinoor-spliced
Crown—
lies at your
resting feet

the Earth
tremors
the Wind
blows
(earthquakes unseen,
unknown...shake the boldest
among the bold...)
but, you
with your eyes closed
smile
(as if
to say):

...this garden
(that grows
a lotus
for Vishnu;
Mayoor-pankh for
Krishna
and manger for a Christ)
had a
rose for me

when i came
blooming, with all its
petals
unfolded
like
a bushel of dreams just
unloaded
...and
then
i planted
a seed...it is
now
a bud
and i have to
leave...

this
is
the
o n l y
w
a
y

thus Life
m
o
v
e
s
a coil of events
interlocked
...and we
tenacious, unflinching
unyielding
(like a family of ants
on a revolving globe)

m o v i n g
and
m
o
v
i
n
g
to probe, seek
and store...

and so
(here, i found a rose
and am leaving a bud
one sunny
day
it will blossom
—you will emerge—)
learn it...)
as a statue carved
on the temple of
Shive
learns...
to think and say:

there are *no*
b
e
g
i
nn
i
n
gs and
no
e
n
d
s
.
.
.

. . .we are (only us)
and our happiness
in
the
seeds
that we plant.

Departure

Lonely and thirsty
the Snow
full
of Spring Desires...

when the Sun was moping
and flowers
waiting
for the gentle rain
to cool-wash their faces
for the
coming Moon

longing to embrace
the trembling grass
(so full of life)
and
flowers and leaves
shimmering
cascading, the Snow
came down

and a hush
fell upon the Earth
All
was Quiet
under that
lip-moistening shroud.

Time stirred, the Watch-Tower
drooping with icicles
shivered, and
the Clock
blinded
croakingly whispered:

"What is more Cruel
than to Desire
those
who cannot
endure
even your touch?"

did the Snow hear! Yes,
perhaps,
for lonely and thirsty, full
of self pity, it slowly
slumped
towards
its
grave

...the gutter...

To a Midnight Dream

Like a sleepy little kitten
captured eyes closed
was i flying on the wings of the black
wind wrapped in leashed
fur and cloistered shoes and
you undated me undamaged and then
you held me in morning light
crowning me while

rain fell outside
our window in diagonal darts and
snow flakes danced around like
reflections of unborn stars
in small calcium fragments
we were

clinging to the inner rings
(they say Saturn has only seven)
but you ought to seek the
eighth and the ninth
(in that sphere that does not
        know how to stand still) and
i threaded the siren songs
with a golden needle so that
the mesmerized Saturn may not
dart dash down on the waiting
warm slippery rocks and
you called me shy! Oh, then
my leashed fur stood-up in the wind
trembling upon my undeciphered body
and danced away the spirituals
and danced away the dumb missiles
and the reins dangled undone
and so did the white bridle
and Saturn rings, colophonied
propelled the blue knots the
cage buttons; the confusion-bars
and the February-five-O'-clock-night
rotated the "round-the-world"
picture-postcards, and in the
mirror of our midnight dream

we tip-toed and swayed like new-born
acorns of wheat dancing in the wild,
the wild west wind,
and we harvested,
we harvested,
and i dreamed what gift
to give you to immortalize
the first morning of my Life.

Tomorrow Is Not Far Away

Because this is Today, Yesterday
          is Not far away...
from two billion B.C. to two billion A.D.
    thoughts interlocked, finger-painting
            the untold history of space.
Forms are many; stations
are trip-weary; and, sometimes
one must sleep.
Seizing that chance,
  a midnight whisper, or a
  morning kiss,
  ties untogetherness a
  Mocking wish...
But, the unwedded knots fray,
  freeze, tear apart
for my fingers may be short,
but yours
        are unsurpassed and
space
    loves to be smothered
up or down or diagonally
when
    there's need to lean upon
from two billion B.C. to two billion A.D.
because you are "you"
         and
  i am   "i,"
Tomorrow
         is Not far away.

Rainbow Knocks at Midnight

Thou hast no sorrow in thy song.
No winter in thy year.
—John Logan, 1748–1788

Late at night someone knocks:
not a wind-blown knight on a
snow-dappled horse, it is
the lame nightingale
singing
one last song, like
a lost rainbow
melting, leaving behind,
a shrouded, bleeding prong.

The song is about old King Frost
—about the lean ghosts he
cut out, stenciled,
leaving behind
eyes like
empty casks.

J'y suis, j'y reste, she hoarsely
calls, "Listen to me, O you
dribbly-droobly, Frost. Bow!
Bow like a thousand gladiators and
cry: O Black Queen!
morituri te salutamus
salutamus..."

She sings, and her darkening wings
shimmer like life-size portraits of
"Now," and *"When,"*
(yesterday's and tomorrow's hollow sails)
smudged, battered and drowning
in the storm-spent, rainbow-carved
sea, bringing half-lit
shadow-memories of Yamaraja's Wings.*

* Yamaraja: the mythical god of Death

My window is of glass. Knocking
sounds fast. "Who is there?"
"Who," mesmerized,
I cry aghast.
"Kuhoo...Kuhoo..."
the fragile partition blasts.

My fingers are freezing. The
window catch breaks, but the
midnight descant
riding the Brutus air
sounds like a Damien chant:
"Come. Come. You must.
There's no other way."

She sings and her dark voice
draping my window, rings:
"Come. Come. Just
give me another push. No,
Not *Tomorrow*, or, *Later*.
But, *Now*. So that, with
my whole Life-thrust, I
can move deeper into and
relish *Today*. Your
fear-worlds—*Yesterday* and
Eternity—
are *nothing* to me.

Her dark eyes spinning the
midnight sky, choke it, make it
mirror-blind. I say: "Go,
from my sky. Go. For I
adore you. I do." And,
for you
I'll join, paste together, the
scattered rainbow-stencils in
their own sun-waves. So that
everyone'll hear
(even the unborn'll whisper):

Even when shorn
of its fractured light,
the phoenix-rainbow
knocks at midnight,
so that Today's blood may *forever* ring,
and the nightingale may *forever* sing.

III
To Let Go...

...They told me, Heraclitus, they told me you were dead;
They brought me bitter news to hear and bitter tears to shed.
I wept, as I remembered, how often you and I
Had tired the sun with talking and sent him down the sky.
And now that thou art lying, my dear old Carian guest,
A handful of grey ashes, long long ago at rest,
Still are thy pleasant voices, they Nightingales awake,
For Death, He taketh all away. but them He cannot take.

—William Johnson Cory, 1823–1892

Silence

bottles of liquid thoughts
corked   sealed   airtight
lie in the center of my courtyard
and too shy to open the cork—
with cracked lips and parched
                                        throat
Silence sits at the edge.

Hope digs a jetty in my backyard
waking Wishes wield spades
the stars hoist shovels
and days crack like stones
nights like clods—
the pier lies empty; the ship of
                                        words
does not reach the shore.

the grounded jetty
    inarticulate without her frigate
stares towards the edge—
like unhappy clods and
injured stones   it
                                waits
                    for the silence
                            to crack

Today

Today
between you and me
darkness
deepens
as it did
before the Atom
was born.

...with the Atom
the world
was born
and then magic
crossed the
Rubicon
—launching
religion and
society and
government;
and rich...and poor

and to fill the gulf,
the sages said:
"suffer not and
pray
for upon darkness
depends
the light of
Life."

...and between you and me
the world was
torn
and
torn
again; for
the darkness
came
and came again.

The Shadow

What a shadow is it that wants to drape me
without any sign of mercy?
Can it be . . . .? Or

Your Memory that i've forgotten? *Yes*. But
your voice
is
the fire
that smolders in the bowels of
the Earth;
and with each tremor, my heart
stands up, trembling in my ears
telling me:

"With a thousand denials carved
upon its undying surface
the heart becomes an eroded
rock
that makes the life's stream flow
thru the corroding world; but,
crumbles
when
touched
by the shadow of a
single word."

What a wave is it that wants to drench me
across a sea of ambushed memories?
It cannot be!
Cannot be!

With—Without

Love:
a manicured fountain
—brilliant in sunlight, and
a vacuum tinctured rainbow
clicking on water
   without it,
switches off with
                    a flick
            of a broken
                    finger-nail.

The Reversed Roles

The earth, we call
"She"
and the sky, "He,"

but
in everyday life i see

it's the "she" who *clouds up* and
rains, and the "he" who
dries up like parched, tearless
dust   when

hung apart
to face
ruthless, endless, supine,
physical quarantine

Which sometimes makes me wonder
  —in our wisdom, rationality
    and all that,
    whose nomenclature
    have we
    bungled-up:
            the Nature's? Or,
            the *Homo sapien's*?

Beyond Understanding

(To my great-grandfather, Raja Hardayal,
who lit up the marching revolt's midnight torch)

It was an evening of riot.
And not understanding the meaning of the revolt,
the taller among the two
was hurt
beyond
understanding...

quivering with rage—
his mind aflame with pain
—he thundered: "I had a gift for you. But
I have changed my mind.
You are above it."

Not waiting to see the impact of his words,
he lashed out again: "Yes, you are
above it.
Above it."

"But...Why?"
wanted to cry
the smaller of the two,
"Can't you *see*? Can't you *understand*!
This revolt is nothing but a reaction
born out of
your
action. This is
Newton's Law. The third one..."

The cry was smothered
by the spreading riot

and in the winds
were words: like images hanging upon
worn threads...

"You Lincoln...You Mighty
        leader of men:
        I had a gift for you—this
        peerless nation of determination. But
        I have changed my mind. You are
        above it. Above it..."
The wind was afraid to carry them. But
they rang.
        Once.
          Twice . .
            Thrice . . .
              WORDS like SHOTS.
                And that was it. For then
                  the winds changed and
                    changed

the images unchanged:
"You Gandhi...You, *Bapu*,
        Bharat-Ratna; *Bharat-Guru*;
        I had a gift for you—this
        eternal land where Gods yearn to love and
        play. But,
        I have changed my mind. You are.
        above it. Above it..."
The wind was afraid to carry them. But.
they rang.
        Once.
          Twice . .
            Thrice . . .
              WORDS like SHOTS.
                And that was it. For then
                  the winds changed and
                    changed

the images unchanged:
"You Kennedy...You, Glorious
        image of American each
        I had a gift for you—this
        land where Love and Liberty like to
          reign. But,
        I have changed my mind. You are
        above it. Above it..."

The wind was afraid to carry them. But
they rang.
Once.
Twice . .
Thrice . . .
WORDS like SHOTS.
And that was it...

and in the winds
were the words: like images hanging
upon worn threads,

quashed
the smaller of the two
closed both eyes
wishing:
there was no roof and
no walls to hang on to;
so that all the weight
could be
borne
by the two
left feet.

The Niagara Falls

how calmly softly this
beauty falls—confident, careless and
                    futile like
torrential rain

                  upon roaring floods; or
                 like
                 stars on a field of
                 dead battle.

This night. This music. This
"Cave of the Winds."
                         Upon
the Rapids is roving
    the "Maid of the Mist."
And
  you are
clashing-tearing within me; i am
bruised and broken with visions:
  A Dark Wood Where
                              Burning
                              Sunlight is
                              Splintered.

Only the Fish

Thrown out of its
water
on the Life's
non-running bank
only the fish
knows
the agony of
death
defying
dreams.

In Tomorrow's *Rouge et Noir*

From out the crystal womb
                          of diamonds
was i thrown
                      into
                              this
                                      burning
                                                      light
to watch forever
                a
                blue
                star   within
a reverie's grasp

Waterproof star looks
                                      d
                                        o
                                          w
                                            n
upon my scalded
face   touching
not
that+=-ambushed
                                rhapsody
lying upon the limpid
pond

O burning blue *
in tomorrow's *rouge et noir*
your eyes will
seek the s
c
a
l
e
s
and
harp-ridden chords
but will see only
the
empty
pond
for today i've made
"forever"
a
word
of
the
past
%+=-

In the Footprints of Nowhere

Her life's Caravan knew *only* a desert,
Where songs were none and fears alert;
Slowly it moved EVER and anon,
And forgotten was the meaning of *Gone.*

But, frolicsome and without fright,
Like an undaunted, cordless kite;
She wandered between day and night,
In a rhythm uncomposed but light.

Then dawned a morn' with polar sheen,
Bringing to light an Oasis green—
A small path ran to a lovely height,
Where lay a *Jewel* precious and bright.

Come on, don't be bashful, it called.
Need a hand, sang the winds enthralled;
Afraid! green grass shook with shock.
Oh, Come on! echoed the rolling hillock.

Fearfully she looked this way and that,
But, images unknown came capering ahead;
And songs long-lost peeling the dread.
Dreamily she stepped on the magic-mat.

????????????????????
!!!!!!!!!!!!!!!!!!!!
&&&&&%%%%%%%%%%%%%%%%
****

But soon came night with
its cringing cap,
And a curtain fell
upon the magician's map;
While the *Mirage*
gleefully laughed *Somewhere*,
Sightless she
stumbled in the
footprints of *Nowhere.*

To the End of the Red-Hot Street

a fawn
cried alone
in a refrigerated jungle...

There were no whispers among the naked trees
where roving shadows touched with silver the
haze blanched blind—
the flesh-color houses surrounded
the empty clearing where no one played;
and there were no Illusions;
no smell of sun;
and a fawn cried alone...

Only the brown sky remembered
the playpen of ideas in carpeted
rooms—the feets of the multitudes

full of Surity and of Memories
of years of walking up and
down
the red-hot street—
reaching no voice and feeling
threatened with Love and Togetherness
that craved to convert the
whole wide world
as one tribe having
one way of walking and one cult...

Did goddess Multiformity—wounded and
bleeding—rose at last and sharpened
Her knife with Her ten toe-nails?

...steel-sparks then
glistened and descended like
showers of quick wrath. The red-hot sky
smothered a sigh—its breath
suffocated; and a brown pallor covered
its scorched face.

...and the jungle was refrigerated
and a fawn
cried alone.

Let the Fire Rage

the Thing
that comes
        with Longing
is *not*
        pain—
it's fire, more fierce
than the one
that burns
        a forest
spreading through
a whole continent
and leaving
in its wake
        only huge limbs
of a red-hot coal
smoldering
under
the mocking eyes of
the eternally revolving
        Sun...

let the Fire rage
for coals
        (even
           the
              smoldering
                 ones)
are better
than
      EMPTINESS.

Unadorned

Last night
Passion shook the naked bench.
Straining emotions,
Kissing the provocative Breeze;
They trembled seeking
Life's honey
  —like prisoners, obsessed
With the Vision
Of closing cell-keys.
Capturing the pregnant flame;
The Memory
Of a challenge
Fixed. Unanswered;
  —*a tableau vivant* (an accident)?
They plunged
Into the traffic-island.

Midnight breaks
No sighs, no tears, no lamentations.
Morning returns.
The traffic
Rotates again
Signs Red and Green
  —blinking, lost
In *Manana* (MIGHT HAVE BEEN). Only
The silent Breeze grieves.
Passion unadorned,
Zigzags in gentle routine.

from Writer's Voice
New York, N.Y.
March 1962

To a Stone Carving

Where has the last December faded!
Why
        December nights
                have submitted to June!

December nights of
warm frost—days full of haze and
zeal
and curvatures
too oblique to unloose—curvatures
which
thru those nights of a December's
                completeness
carved a life of
                Foreverness
on a thermal stone.

Where has the last December faded?
                Why December nights
have submitted to June? To June
...to these days of
   empty suns and hollow moons...
to these stone-eyed days
whose breath
                i fear
not because they are of a
                brightness
that hurts like a nightmarish
                ice-hot awakening;
not because their
                single-mindedness
adds strange symphonies to the
                last requiem for
                Foreverness...
but because i know what's gone is
                                gone and
nothing ever returns except
                                a boomerang
                                or
                                a memory.

To Remember

(To all my friends at
International House, New York City)

At this moment of parting
let me present you
something

...pretty
that you'll always treasure
and will never loan to anyone.
A gift

...of past present and future
that'll give you a longing to live
and to create things beautiful.
Eternal

...again and again
you'll look at it and say,
"Ah! What Happiness! What Joy!
in the years

...to come and gone-by
in this universe I'm the one,
the only one
to own

...this token of unspoken love,
a pearl hidden in its shell
an unshed tear."

IV
To Go With…

…There's a long, long trail awinding
Into the land of my dreams,
Where the nightingales are singing
And a white moon beams:
There's a long, long night of waiting
Until my dreams all come true,
Till the day when I'll be going down
That long, long trail with you.

—Stoddard King, 1889–1933

Sound without End

Soft
are rose petals;
                clouds
over *Kanchanjanga;*

the stealing steps of a new
                morn'
and the sound
                of
                the door
                opened by your hand.

Door to the Deep Ocean

Door to the deep ocean...Open,
lead me thru thy corridors
where amid light green weeds lie
ruins of gallant boats dreaming
like the scattered pearls
of a kidnapped bride

...where the stars
are the bridesmaids;
Moon,
the best man
and the Sun
softly treads, like
a suffering knight

where under the ruins and the sea-weeds
slumbers peace deep and affluent as
sleep that comes to children
every night
when their closed eyes give them the
sight to reach out for f a r away
things and unite, without
shame or fright

Door to the deep ocean...Open
lead me now
as the winds lead honey-bee
to a blossom
far away and pearly white.

The Man Named Yesterday

the man named Yesterday
stands
with a rod in his hand
and with his smooth, shiny gloves
points
        the *Way* one must take:

"*This is* the Path. The One.
the Only One," he sings,
smiles his sleek smile; and
chants, "Straight Ahead...

                "Straight ahead you must
walk; and never be misled.
For the straight path
is the *only* path that can
give
    you
        Salvation, Joy
            (and on top of that)
        Freedom from God's wrath."

the woman named Tomorrow
sits with her mouth gagged and
wrings her chained hands:
        "Oh! Young 'ne! *Young One*!

"You, who have taken
Yesterday's advice, and
are walking
on your wobbly legs—
don't be blind. Open your
eyes and look...

"Look, you are treading upon
antiquated, raw eggs.
for the straight path is not
so great. Its aching back
is a moth-eaten
                    bridge that
cannot
bear a single crack...

"No, Young One.
      No, my darling, Present,
  the *straight path* is not
always *the* best
for when suddenly
        (without any wink or
warning), the crack comes,
it leaves under your feet
nothing...

"Nothing.
      Not a single plank.
            Not a single peg."

Sense or Nonsense

" Babes in the wood are we,"
    cry Friendship and Liberty.
" The paths are jumbled. They
  don't make sense
  in this
maze of passions dubbed
    —*I*ntegrity or
      *N*yctalopia
      *D*iscipline (and No. 3)
      *I*ntoxication (No. 4)
      *V*enality (and...)
      *I*njustice (plus...)
      *D*ishonesty
      *U*nity
      *A*ntagonism (and)
      *L*ove (...)
their primal petals
stand in a row
and conjugate to
reveal
a shackled enigma
        The
        individual."

An Ode to Our Heartland

(Poem for the day i decided to be an American)

LIFE—a chain of gene-propelled, Trinity-compelled
    self-seeking Plasma
—blind. Earth-bound. Kaleidoscopic
beyond comprehension...and, in its Time-cuffed
links
are many (who, for one reason or another)
lose their anchor. Their Gods. And, then wish
to re-find (HIM. THEM. ANYONE)
like first-borns
                    re-seeking
                    their natural
                                    womb.
                                                    Oh! Did you
hear about him? That cruel, self-loving, unholy
*thug**, who six-thousand years ago roamed
the retreating jungles looting weary travellers
but came a day throwing in his red eyes
an ode to the new morning chimed
in a deep tenor by a baby-brown sparrow
silenced suddenly
by a hunter's arrow, and that unfinished song,
those unsung notes hovered, closed upon him,
following him everywhere till in Death and
Pain he found the reason why
the earth round and round revolved
so endlessly, searchlighting, pinpointing
the images of unchanging RAMA.
                                                    So, he
changing
his name to Valmiki
wrote the *Ramayana*

* killer-robber

not knowing
that he, the very first human poet,
was laying down laws eternal
for millions of self-proclaimed Aryans
(Hindus), for billions of years to come
and, then,
centuries later Shelley read him
and stated the axiom "Poets are Unacknowledged
Legislators Of The World."
Are, they?
Yes, perhaps
for the world is moved not
by mind-boggling armaments
but
by ideas
unlost and unwavering
like the *Valmiki Himalayas*

(..."The Himalayas," said six-year-old Soma,
"are in the North. I'll bring them South.")

"How," asked papa Shyam Lal, "and, Why?"

"Simple," said the ever-inquisitive
engineer's daughter, "I'll move India North,
then the Himalayas'd be to our South...and,
you know what, Papa, the *Gurkhas*,
hating the alien heat,
believing it's the British who did it,
would drown them in dear-old
Cape Camorin."
"Don't build dream-castles.
Build bridges on this earth," chided softly,
British India's patriotic,
chair-chained, officer.

and
in the Lion's own den, Elizabeth Browning
sang
"The Cry Of Children," and, forced
Lord Peele to pass legislation banning
employment of helpless
children under indecent
conditions.
Oh, Yes!
It does happen...the poet only
sows the seeds, but reaps
high-noon whirlwind
...did you hear Byron in Greece...those
Olympus-thundering words which gave the
Greeks
strength to drive out the Turks...
Oh, Yes!
Generations
come and vanish
with their footprints
the laws enacted
by elected-legislators benumb,
branded unsuitable.
Obsolete.
And, there are rebellions against
the unjust, obsolete laws, and they are
repealed, but,
unconcerned,
the poet sings
like his
solitary nightingale knocking at
tomorrow's Dawn
even when he is
misquoted,
misunderstood...did you
ever hear
even in those glorified, jungle days,
when the "White Man's Burden"
was
"Oh, East is East and West is
West, and never the twain
shall meet..." that's not all.
Kipling *had also*
mournfully, stated:

"But, there is neither East nor
West. Border, nor Breed, nor birth, when
two strong men stand face to face, though they
come from the ends of the earth."*

A link
can close its ears,
but, the Chain hears
for the Poet
is the unseen Master of puppets,
sliding in
games in the mighty parliaments,
dreampainting
his cannons
and his slow-burning
ideas
travel with Bread, Light, and Water on the
wings of Time-winds
as that
inevitable Shelley
so aptly said:
"Drive my dead thoughts
over the universe
Like withered leaves
to quicken a new birth!
And by the incantation
of this verse
Scatter, as from an
extinguished hearth,
Ashes and sparks, my
words among mankind."
A chain, needs
no incarnation,
just a new link...Robert Frost,
"THIS LAND WAS OURS," thundered he,
"BEFORE WE WERE OF THE LAND..."
and his tenor echoed, stationed images
in every home on the roving earth so that
all may re-know
how easy it is in the
engulfing Life

* From Kipling's *Truce of the Bear,* stanza 2

to lose
your horizons, and
how easy
to re-find them
when you are true to Life
and to Yourself.
And, thus in the trail of
Saint Valmiki, the first known poet
of God's earth-born,
follow those who refind
their Love, their Dreams,
their Heartland...On the shifting
sands of Time, they anchor like a *Kauri*,*
unknown, uncared for, and timeless.
Timeless, and building dream-bridges
linking
today's
crawling, baby technologies
to tomorrow's misty, mind-boggling,
space-shattering Himalayas.
And, it
will always be so
for like unsung sparrow notes, they are
uncut
diamonds
hidden in the eternal republic-womb
not-needing-not wanting
opium recognition.
Only wanting to sing along in unhushed,
unbridled, notes, such as,
Edna St. Vincent Millay's
Time-toting words:
"The world stands out
on either side
no wider than the heart is
wide...
the heart can push the sea
and land
farther away on either
hand..."

* seashell

Ode to the Four-Year-Old

for him today
a spade is a magic-blade
to build sand-castles.

and POLITICS a word unheard.
ECONOMICS, a penny
                                to buy a bird.
POWER? inalienable caliber
to cast anchor
upon little sister's honey-
    sweet hair. SPACE SHIPS?
they also exist as interesting
do-it-yourself stuff-on-a-chair.

there's *work* too. Oh, yes. it
is skill and strength
                                to imitate
the father, who is so great
that he is not afraid
of the mighty
                                shaving blade.

BUT, when *tomorrow* comes
        it'll be a strange world
—PEOPLE: yellow, black and white;
  MARKETS: FLUNG FROM OCEAN TO
  OCEAN; AND SPIRES OF INDUSTRIES
  SPANNING to unite; science shoving
  in new walls to imprison the Man,
  who'll then be the mighty MACHINE
  ruled by SCHEMING robots working
          from nine to five.

in this new world,
a spade will be a *spade*;
and castles,
crowns to be ignored or
                    overthrown.

before it's too late will someone
gather together
those entombed
thoughts and efforts, which are still
sucking in feeble breaths, and
shape them into something like
magic wands
to transform today's world into one
that would offer
        today's four-year-olds
        a little more than just the
                blank word—*future*.

It Needs Only Two

My daughter,
Light of my eyes, says my
  ayah (she's
  very brave and bright),
this is the age
  of satellites, of
  nuclear bombs,
  and
  people who have any
  wits,
  are dubbed, 'Eggheads'
  or, 'parasites'...
Your generation—mind you,
i'm not a pessimist
—but, i won't be surprised
  if your generation is
  the last one to bask
  in our capricious God's
  spaceship's
  living sunlight...

My papa's Mummy winks
  (she does not read or
  write.
  But, oh! You should
  see her wrinkled
  eyes. They're so
  sunny-funny and
  erudite as if
  full of dynamite. And
her winsome, toothless
smile...it evokes in
our minds, such a
  volcanic delight...)

Come she says,
let's go to bed, my child.

You're
afraid? But, why? Look,
this horizon that you
see day and night
...where does it end and
why? What is the Sun; the
Moon; the stars? And What
lies beyond
the distant skies?...

...these are *also*
the questions
that throbbed in man's mind
in those days
which are now dubbed
—the Dark Ages.

But,
in those days, Man's mind
was embryonic
—like an
un-hewn patch of a fertile
mine...for, you see, the
world was very young then,
and man
was her crawling baby
...crawling unaided...
on the dark, steep, mounting
slopes of
menacing shadows
lighted only by
restless flares of
greasy fright.

And,
to secure himself tight, he
thoughtfully,
carefully,
entwined knotted, unyielding
ropes of devotion, faith and
credulous, self-perpetuating
doctrines...

Making,
Sun the symbol of power;
Moon of romance and poetry;
Rainbow a bridge
to catch a sweetheart's eyes;
and *Learning* a goddess
        to be pleased
        by putting at her holy feet
        each new invention,
        such as,
                a new flower, a
                fruit, or tasty
                sweets...

The questions of those
days, glowing like a
    tapering candle-light,
have now become
    bold and bright, like
    the nose of a telescopic
searchlight
    hovering to reach
    some unfathomed height.

                        So you see,
        my child, there's
        nothing to fear.
Science is *only*
the first primer, the
        A...B...C...D
        of the law of nature
and man's rocking efforts
are only signs of his
        adolescence and
        awakening.

...the awakening that once
made the man hammer the
nail, and shape the wheel,
        plough the earth,
        draw water, and
        invent,
        manufacture
        things like,
                wheat, barley
                and rice...

And, for centuries to come,
everyone
can smile and proclaim:
   won't you remember,
   now, and for ever...the
   progress of science
   does not mean
destruction of man by his
own kind. Our forefathers
were crazy for Power. Sure.
They were brave and rash,
   ready to offend and fight.
   But, any day, any hour,
   any night, they were not
—not for a second—
incapable
            of loving, or
            living...

So, my baby-darling,
   may you also
   grow up to be
a scientist—enquiring,
               itching,
               laboring,
               thundering,
               floundering,
to discover
breathless secrets
that since the
Dark Ages

in Man's abundant
laboratories
have given birth
to:
breathless music,
plays, crying out and
never-ending stories
—all,
simple products
of this groping thing,
called:
Knowledge
—the goddess of learning,
or,
Saraswati.
Listen to the air. It
whistles
Her songs.
And in the songs, there's
a message:
"Remember,
as long as, we
have this earth, and the
Sun, and the Moon, and the
stars (our atom-structured
chariot, with its untiring
wheels),
our feelings
seeded
in our poetry—our knowledge,
will
not
die...
"Therefore,
do not forget—today, or
any tomorrow,
—the caveman
had only his wife, but he
was not afraid, when he
discovered
the Power

of
poison and fire…
"Even he (such a fallible
baby though he was
of Future and
Eternity),
knew…well understood…
that the *club of knowledge*
must be acquired
for *club* is Power…
club is Understanding
and *understanding is Love*,
the *raison d'etre* of life.
…and that (anytime):
it needs *only* two
for poetry to be born for
this universe to continue
as it might…"

To Julie and Jim

who'll say why in their own sphere
are born two—never to fulfill each
                    other

for living like ever always
—strangers in a trillion-billion ways
there was a Julie
and there was a Jim
and the first time when she saw him
standing near a chair
    (one foot up, the other down
    on inquisitive lips, a pencil brown)
rooted, transfixed, she was. Her hand
trembled on the threshold's knob
    (was it "Love at First Sight?
    No. Modern girls DON'T
        believe in THAT")

    "Stop fighting Life," her tingling
limbs cried. "But, I can't."
"You must. Centuries old is your armour.
Don't let it chain you for ever."

    "Nice meeting you," he said:
but she was confused and bewildered.
    "Pardon?"
"Nice meeting you, I said."
    "Oh! Nice meeting you," she
breathed and fled.

winds howl
    skies weep
Where are you Destiny? An
aching electrode cries:
    "Are you
        totally blind; or
            just drunk?"

but fate holds to his grounds and smiles
two parallel lines
never meet—they say.
in abstract yes.
but in real life they do
sometimes

for wheels of life
keep on
turning.

That Night

That night.
  Those stars.
and under the trees—
those steps slow
                    tight
                    together
walking.

"Life *is* Funny..."
  (did i say that!)
"Life is Interesting..."
  (did you
            smile
                    like
                         that!)

Then
a moonbeam fell and
cut the feet
in two and two

i'm
     still
     wondering: WHICH
            tightness
            is true!

Until

They told me:
Sunlight is beautiful
(pure and divine)
with power to heal
even
the deepest wounds
and

anytime, anywhere
it is
the only nectar
Life needs
to live

BUT
i did not know the meaning
of these words
until
i saw
your face

No Matter How Many Time-Curtains

Through the shimmering, crystal curtains
some moon-rays
come sliding in, tuning up
the loneliness
    that reigns on
the mutinous memory-player,
humming the window panes into
    mirrors of fine music
    and, reflecting
        the unfinished Descartes,
the man—(or, "God yours,"
said your past-tense-clay-smeared
fingers sculpting the eleventh commandment)
that knew when lost
one should leave like a
    straight line.
You never heard the one
descant that all my shadows
    mount on the Moon-rays:
    "Shape me, O God, make me,
        a whisper of Wind,
so I could ruffle your hair
and touch your hand
    no matter
    how many
        Time-curtains between us."

A Song for Sunlight

Saturday morning
seeping through the sleeping window
sunlight writes
new songs
with graphs of kisses
and inks of love
    —beating rhythm
on an anchored
budding bough

Saturday morning
seeping through the sleeping window
morning air floats
through word-whisperings
and the new song
        takes wings
to spread upon
the distant hillocks—
    Your words:
        a waterfall
        billowing and spilling
        thru the sky into
        the earth
            or
                running warmth

(From Poet *magazine*
Madras, India
Jan.–Feb. 1966)

Nightingale Needs No Sidewalks

Sidewalks
safe, sturdy, unlittered with
        Life's tangled
        scorpion webs.
If one sidetracked from
one's blind midstream
        wanders by
desiring
        another, who
just lightly steps aside
letting the seeker,
the lonely stumbler,
droopingly
        move on, or,
linger behind.

BUT,
the Lion keeps roaring
   in the Mango grove
not even stirring the
        divine, myth-moths,
just trampling on
marking
        new paths.

Sidewalks
shielded, smooth, unslippery
        stationed carefully
        at the Bethlehem
of Life, like shadows living
non-breathing, non-hungry
under the Morning-candle
seducing Death with their
undying, mocking breath
        to invite
        her Beethovan kiss
at their pre-Raphaelite,
daylight dazzling mind.

BUT,
the Peacock keeps dancing
   in the Mango grove
not even trampling upon
just tip-toeing around
the crow-carcass of
customs dead and gone.

Sidewalks
deserts, chilled, unmoving
         seeded perennially
         by singing sunlight.
Empty early-morning, empty
midnight, except for some
invisible, fickle fingers
silvermounting gyrating
graffiti lines:
         "If the Sky does not
loosen his liquid arms, Earth's
steaming breath does not rise
arching, and the Rainbow dies
in Indrani's*
               locked womb."

BUT,
the baby nightingale's
time-splitting songs
        keep ringing in
the the new Dawn chilled
Sidewalk-disdaining
              Mango grove.

In our new cuckoo-morning
There's no room for "MAY-BE YES,"
         No room for "MAY-BE NO."
We shall walk
              those Sidewalks
                                        NO MORE.

* *Indrani*: consort of Lord Indra, the rain-God.

Little Bit India—Little Bit U.S.A.

(To my friends in A.I.A. Inc.)

My song is your song
  Your song is mine
O', let our song go
  Across our waiting ravine

  —our mind has two doors
    one in great-old-Bombay
    one in great-old-N.Y.
Music is India; Music U.S.A.
          I'm a little bit India
            little bit U.S.A.

My dance is your dance
  Your dance is mine
O', let our dance mesmerize
        Our linking ravine

  —our music has two doors
    one in legacy-draped Delhi
    and one in dreamy L.A.
Freedom is India; Freedom U.S.A.
          I'm a little bit India
            little bit U.S.A.

My hope is your hope
  Your hope is mine
O', let our hopes twine
  Bridging our waiting sky

  —our love has two doors
    one in dear-old-India
    one in dear-old-U.S.A.

'Coz our love has two doors
    one in dear-old-India
    one in dear-old-U.S.A.

O', old is India and new U.S.A.
      I'm a little bit old
    and a little bit new
          a little bit India
  and a little bit U.S.A.

Voila Tout

(To my father, late Shri Shyam Lal, I.S.E.)

Outside my window darkness reigns—

The rustle of Aspen trees can be heard
            far away, it feels
as if this night'll never be another day;

and under the dark shadows
    i can sense
              some twigs
twisted and bent
  as if passionately kissed
            by the looming death-winds.

Under the wind's deep shadows lie the days
when I was a tiny twig
adult-lies shielded
not told
what happens to those
who hunger
            to harness
hard-hitting, sun-sapping,
            time-leaping
                      Badvanals.*

But, now Finally,
                i'm a Banyan
full-blossomed,
solid, unshielded,
                and able to endure

* Forest fire.

the rustle of Knowledge. It feels
there's something that
cannot be learned,
geared, granted,
until the end,
until the final skins are dropped,
when
we surrender and
accept the blow that stings
like a whisper
of a river-eroded Neem:

—here and now
we are
on today's edge
hugging
the lost waters,
the dream-titanics
those never-neverland
existent,
optative,
pre-determined and
so polychromatic,
unlost Pompeiis

while knowing
savouring all the time
the ghosts
of those fragile, white paper-boats
that sailed the still lake
will rise
only as the Captains of
moon-bound,
burnished-steel
space-time ships.

Yes. Despite
all its perseverance,
Life f
a
l
l
s. It Only
Postpones

defeat on this Shiva-Durga's Planet.
It's True. Very-Very-True.
But,
Roots remain.
Roots Remember. They Do.
So, Baby, you,
Stride the Future.
Keep riding the River.
Holding the two River-Banks together
so the twain will meet
thru You.
Voila Tout.